W9-AXP-398

THE PLAGUE

BY JONATHAN HARLEN

ILLUSTRATED BY TOM JELLETT

COVER ILLUSTRATION BY DAVID PALUMBO

Librarian Reviewer
Marci Peschke
Librarian, Dallas Independent School District
MA Education Reading Specialist, Stephen F. Austin State University
Learning Resources Endorsement, Texas Women's University

Reading Consultant
Elizabeth Stedem
Educator/Consultant, Colorado Springs, CO
MA in Elementary Education, University of Denver, CO

STONE ARCH BOOKS
Minneapolis San Diego

First published in the United States in 2008
by Stone Arch Books
151 Good Counsel Drive, P.O. Box 669
Mankato, Minnesota 56002
www.stonearchbooks.com

First published in Australia in 1996 by Lothian Books
(now Hachette Livre Australia Pty Ltd)

Published in arrangement with Hachette Livre Australia.

Library of Congress Cataloging-in-Publication Data
Harlen, Jonathan, 1963–
[Carriers]
The Plague / by Jonathan Harlen; illustrated by Tom Jellett.
p. cm. — (Shade Books)
Summary: When Will is bitten on his arm by a weird pet store owner and becomes ill, no one believes that has been afflicted with a fatal disease.
ISBN-13: 978-1-59889-861-3 (library binding)
ISBN-10: 1-59889-861-2 (library binding)
ISBN-13: 978-1-59889-917-7 (paperback)
ISBN-10: 1-59889-917-1 (paperback)
[1. Horror stories.] I. Jellett, Tom, ill. II. Title.
PZ7.H22653Pl 2008
[Fic]—dc22 2007003729

Art Director: Heather Kindseth
Graphic Designer: Kay Fraser

1 2 3 4 5 6 12 11 10 09 08 07

Printed in the United States of America

TABLE OF CONTENTS

Chapter 1

Brinkley's Wild Kingdom of Pets

A wildcat was in the window of the store.

It was caged inside a box the size of a TV set. The box had stiff wires across the front. The bottom of the box was covered with straw, and there was a hole cut in the back for air.

The cat, which was only slightly larger than a house cat and very thin, lay stretched out. Its eyes were closed. It was napping in the early morning sun.

There was a girl on the sidewalk outside the store. She stood perfectly still. Her black hair was in a ponytail, and a dark blue backpack was over her shoulder.

As she looked in through the window, tears filled her eyes. They stayed there for a minute, and then spilled down her cheek.

The girl breathed as the tears slid down to her jaw.

A boy walked up next to her. He was carrying a backpack, too.

He was about a foot taller than the girl. His face was stretched in a wide grin.

He said, "Melissa! Melissa, you just missed your bus! Didn't you hear it? What are you doing?"

He stopped when he noticed that she was crying. Her eyes were red. He stopped talking and let his smile fade. Then he moved forward and placed a hand on her shoulder.

"Hey, what's the matter? You okay?" he asked gently.

"No, I'm not okay," Melissa said angrily.

"What's wrong? Is it this? The store?" the boy asked.

"Yes. I hate it. I hate it!" Melissa pointed toward the window. "All those wild animals. They're not pets."

The boy looked at the wildcat, and at the other animals caged in the window. There was a ferret, a lizard, and a coiled snake.

He pointed above the door. "Well, it says they are on the sign. Brinkley's Wild Kingdom of Pets." He smiled.

He waited until Melissa wiped her eyes. His name was Will Noonan, and he had known Melissa for three years.

His parents had moved to Green Valley from the city, to get away from smog and crime and overcrowding.

Will's father still drove to the city every day for work. He drove an hour and a half along the freeway.

Green Valley was a small suburban town. The ground was flat as a pancake, and the town was on the edge of a big brown desert called the Wash.

Green Valley was supposed to be some kind of paradise, but most of the time Will was bored out of his mind.

"The cat is so thin," Melissa said, pointing at the window. "Look. The owner can't be feeding it right."

Will looked closely at the wildcat.

"Yeah, you can see all its ribs and stuff," he agreed. "It looks like it's starving."

"The ferret looks like it's starving too," Melissa said angrily. "It's awful. The owner shouldn't be allowed to treat them like that."

Will pictured the owner of the store in his mind.

Mr. Brinkley was a strange old man. He was fat and balding, and had a scar on the side of his neck.

There was a message stuck on the door in shaky black handwriting: CLOSED DUE TO ILLNESS. The window was dark, but there was movement behind the glass.

Will reached forward and tried the door handle. The door opened.

"I tell you what," he said. "If we find somebody inside, I'll buy it for you. The wildcat. Then we'll take it down to the Wash and set it free."

Melissa blinked. "Buy it for me?" she said.

Will shrugged. "Yeah. I've got some money. Why not? It'll be fun. We could buy some food for it, too. What do you think?"

Melissa smiled. "Sure. I'd like that. But can we go in there? The sign says it's closed."

Will shrugged again. "The guy's in there right now. I saw him moving around. And the door's open. Let's go."

Will headed into the store. Melissa hesitated, and then followed him.

CHAPTER 2

BITTEN

It was dark inside. The owner was nowhere to be seen. There were only the animals, in cages lining the walls.

As he got used to the light, Will realized just how many animals there were in the small store. He saw at least a dozen more wildcats. He also saw ferrets, lizards, and snakes, and parrots in a birdcage.

Several of the parrots were lying face down on the bottom of their cage. They looked dead. So did some of the lizards and ferrets. Not a single creature was moving.

The smell in the shop was awful. It was a sick, hot smell.

The animals that looked dead could be dead, Will realized. They were dead, or sick, or dying. Something was wrong.

He turned to look at Melissa and they began to back away, toward the open door behind them, and daylight.

Then the owner, Mr. Brinkley, appeared at the back of the shop.

As he came into the light they could see him more clearly. He was carrying a plastic dish filled with water. With each step that he took, water spilled.

"No time," he whispered to himself. "No time. Must give. Must . . . give . . ."

When he saw the two people in the store, he straightened up a little. A strange light came into his eyes. "No!" he said. "The door! You can't come in!"

"It was open," Will said slowly. He was frozen to the spot. "Are you all right? Do you need any help?"

The man stood up straighter. His whole body was shaking. Water from the plastic dish spilled everywhere.

"Help me," the man whispered. "Help!"

Another sigh escaped him. He tried to speak but could not. He fell to the floor.

Melissa grabbed Will's elbow. "Let's get out of here!"

Will stepped toward the man and reached down to touch his shoulder.

"He's sick, Melissa. He needs an ambulance! Go call 911!" he yelled. "Hurry up! There must be a phone, right? Maybe in the back."

Melissa shrieked, “Will, look out!”

Will turned in time to see the man standing up. The light in his eyes was wild. His teeth were bared. Before Will could move, the old man leaped forward.

His mouth locked onto Will’s right arm. He bit down hard into the flesh below Will’s elbow, breaking the soft skin.

Will yelled and dropped his backpack. With his left hand, he pushed the man hard in the side of the head.

The man’s mouth loosened immediately, and his jaw fell open. The man slid to the floor.

Will stepped backward, holding on to his arm. He could see blood trickling down between his fingers.

"Melissa!" Will said. "He bit me!"

"Let's get out of here," Melissa said.

"He bit me," Will cried. "Look at my arm!"

"Will, please, let's go," Melissa begged. "This is horrible. Please."

Some of the birds had begun twittering in their cages. A wildcat perched near the ceiling let out a yowl.

Will picked up his backpack and turned toward the door. A stab of pain shot through his arm. He looked down at his arm again and saw a row of deep marks, dark and swelling below his elbow.

With Melissa just ahead of him, he stumbled out of the store.

CHAPTER 3

THE WASH

Will's fever began two hours later. They'd gone to Melissa's house to take care of Will's arm.

The pain was almost gone by the time they got to Melissa's, although the bite marks were still swollen.

Melissa cleaned the bite marks and put some kind of cream on them.

Then she bandaged Will's arm.

They didn't talk much about what had happened. It was too weird and creepy.

Will had a headache, and didn't feel like going to school.

They couldn't stay at Melissa's because her mother came home from work after lunch.

So they decided to walk to the Wash.

The Wash was the last undeveloped land in Green Valley.

Everything else had been bought and built on, but not the Wash.

The Wash had mostly been left alone.

The Wash stretched between the sports complex and the civic center, and then past the country club. It divided the town into two parts.

It was the place the older kids went on weekends and after school.

The Wash was the place Will went, too, whenever he wanted to get away.

"You have to be careful. There's broken glass around here," he said to Melissa as they climbed down the bank.

"Yuck," Melissa said.

"Lizards, too," Will added. "In the holes under the rocks. And scorpions, sometimes."

They walked along the stony, dried-up riverbed.

They were approaching the storm drain on the far bank. Then Will turned around quickly. He stared up the hill to his left, into a grove of trees.

"What was that?" Will asked.

Melissa shrugged. "I don't know. I didn't see anything."

"I heard something," Will said. "It sounded like it was some kind of animal."

He wasn't sure exactly what he had heard. A rustling somewhere? Something growling? Or nothing at all?

As he walked along the dry riverbed, he felt sweat on his forehead. There was also pounding in the back of his head. His headache was getting worse.

"It's hot," he said.

"Are you all right?" Melissa asked. "Maybe you should go to a doctor."

"Nah," Will said. "I'm hot, that's all. Let's get into the shade."

They walked to where the storm drain stuck out from the bank. The drain, and the thick concrete pillars that held it up, were covered in graffiti. A ditch had been carved into the earth under it, where the storm water flowed away.

Will had the feeling that someone, or something, was following him. Something watching, only a short distance away. It was waiting.

He looked back, up the bank into the bushes. Nothing. He moved out of the shade for a moment, and the sun beat down, hotter than before. A sudden wave of sickness came over him.

"I think I'm going to be sick," Will said.

Melissa looked alarmed. "Sick?"

Will whispered, "Yeah, sick. I'm . . ." With a croak, he threw up onto the rocks.

The pounding in Will's head had started to go away, but he felt weaker, and hotter than ever. Maybe he'd gotten what the old man had, whatever that was.

Melissa stood up. "You need to get home," she told him.

Will wiped his mouth. "No, I'm all right. It's just some kind of bug."

"You need to see a doctor. You look terrible," Melissa said. She sounded worried.

Will slowly got to his feet.

He didn't want to leave the Wash so soon. He wanted to show Melissa how you could use sticks to scare lizards out of their holes in the rock, and how giant yellow butterflies came down sometimes to perch on the branches of the trees.

He had to see the doctor. He was feeling pretty sick. There was no doubt about that.

Chapter 4

Something Strange

Will's mother worked in a dress store in the town's biggest shopping mall.

The store was near the food court of the mall. Will had only been there a few times. He hated malls and shopping, and his mom didn't like having him there anyway.

Mrs. Noonan was worried about losing her job. She had told Will many times not to come into the store, because he was always dirty and she was afraid he would embarrass her.

Today, though, he was sick.

He needed his mother's help. There was nobody else he could ask.

Melissa carried Will's backpack for him as far as the mall entrance.

She couldn't go inside with him because she was supposed to be at school.

So Will went in alone.

The effort of walking up from the Wash and across the park had brought his headache back worse than before.

His entire body was burning, from his ears to the tips of his toes. He wasn't sweating, though, which was strange. Not a drop, not even on his forehead.

Behind him, again, he sensed something. It was something silent and hidden. It was watching.

That feeling had been with him ever since they had arrived at the Wash.

He had sensed it move as soon as he stood up.

It was almost as if the something had moved and started paying attention to Will.

It was impossible that anything could be following him, but something was.

He was sure.

Was it possible that he had imagined it?

Maybe it was just his mind playing tricks on him.

As Will walked into his mother's store, he was sure everything would be all right.

His mother would take him to the doctor, and the doctor would give him some medicine.

He would go home, get a good night's sleep, and be good as new.

Inside the store his mother was talking to a woman in a hat.

The woman was standing in front of a mirror, pushing her fingers in at her waist, admiring a skirt.

When Mrs. Noonan saw Will, her face looked upset.

She muttered something to her customer and walked over quickly to meet Will at the doorway.

"What are you doing here?" she whispered. "I thought I told you not to come in here! Why aren't you at school?"

"I don't feel good," Will said. "I think I'm sick."

"Oh, for heaven's sake." She stared at him. "What kind of sick?"

"I have a fever. My arm got bitten," Will explained.

"Playing down in the Wash again, no doubt. Look at you, you're covered in dirt," his mother said angrily.

Will stared at the carpet.

There was no point trying to explain.

Will had the feeling his mother wouldn't believe him anyway. She never seemed to believe anything he said, not anymore.

Besides, he was beginning to feel dizzy.

"I threw up, Mom," he said. "I feel awful. I need to get to a doctor."

His mom sighed. "Well, you'll just have to wait until my lunch break. I'll take you to the doctor then. Wait in the back, where no one can see you."

For the next hour, Will sat, shivering, in the storeroom.

He threw up once more into an empty box.

Then he got up and looked at himself in the mirror.

He was pale, and his hair was strangely limp, almost as if it were wet. But when he touched it, his hair was dry and crackly, like straw.

The rest of the time he spent looking around the room. He peered between the piles of boxes and the dress racks under the tables, even up at the ceiling.

It was crazy. There was nothing in the room except clothes and a bunch of boxes. However, the thing that had followed him was still with him. He knew it.

At one o'clock his mother came in. She took him to their family doctor, Dr. Finster, whose office was at a nearby clinic.

Dr. Finster checked Will's eyes and throat, felt his chest and stomach, and listened to his heart. When he finished, he looked puzzled.

"There's nothing really wrong with you, as far as I can tell," he said. "Your temperature's a little high, but your pulse is fine. You threw up this morning, right?"

Will nodded.

"He's been playing down in the Wash again," his mother said. "He goes there after school. We've tried everything to stop him. His teachers have talked to him. The police have talked to him. He knows it's dangerous, but he keeps going."

Dr. Finster nodded. "It is dangerous, certainly. There's very little shade down there at all. And if you were out in that sun for more than a couple of hours, after throwing up your breakfast, it's no wonder you feel sick. No wonder at all."

Will's brain was foggy, his head was spinning, but he forced himself to speak. "I didn't throw up my breakfast. And it wasn't the sun. It's something else. There's something following me."

His mother frowned. "Oh, Will, for heaven's sake."

"There is!" Will cried. "Since I got bitten! Look at my arm!"

He held up his hurt elbow. Dr. Finster took it in one hand and began unwrapping the bandage.

"So you got bitten, huh?" the doctor said. "What bit you? A dog? A snake?"

"No, not an animal. A man. A man bit me," Will replied.

"A man bit you!" Dr. Finster raised his eyebrows. "Well, now. I don't see too many bites like that. Let's take a look."

He continued to unwrap the bandage. Suddenly Will felt like the thing that was following him was there. The feeling was stronger than ever before. There had to be some sign of it in the room.

He sat up, his heart pounding, his breath trapped in his throat, just as the doctor lifted the last piece of the bandage away.

The bite marks on his arm were gone.

The place where the ugly, swollen bite marks had been was now perfectly healthy skin. Nothing. No injury at all.

Will stared in disbelief. He looked at the bandage in the doctor's hands. It was white, no trace of blood. As clean as if it had never been used.

He got to his feet, trembling. He could feel the thing moving behind him. He could almost sense the shape of it. The smell. The gaze burning into his shoulders.

Will spun around, screaming. The doctor grabbed him by the shoulders. Will broke free and ran.

He ran out of the office, down the hall, and out to the parking lot, where he jumped into his mother's car. He didn't dare look behind him.

Chapter 5

A Black Cloud

Will went to bed early, but he woke up in the night. He felt like something was trying to get inside him. His blood felt like it was crawling, like a line of ants. He was weak. He was burning up. His pillow was dry, though, and when he put his hand to his forehead, he wasn't sweating.

After he fell back asleep, he had a nightmare. A black cloud settled just above his face, tickling his nose and mouth. Each time he breathed he sucked more of the cloud into his lungs.

Will woke up coughing several times. He kept feeling like the cloud was still in the room.

Once he even thought he heard it moving, like the whispering of a desert wind, somewhere over by the curtains.

The next morning his mother took his temperature. It was normal. She told him to go to school but he refused.

He was so weak he could hardly walk down the stairs. The thought of eating breakfast made him want to throw up.

Finally, his mother stormed off to work and left him at home alone for the day. He lay on the couch watching TV, dozing on and off. His whole body ached.

The next day he stayed home again. He ate some breakfast, and managed to hold it down, but he still felt weak.

His mother took him back to Dr. Finster, who examined him a second time.

The doctor couldn't find anything wrong. "A good night's sleep, that's what he needs!" Dr. Finster said. "And a good meal. Maybe even a steak."

That was the last straw, as far as Will's mother was concerned.

"You're faking this whole thing, aren't you?" she snapped at Will as they drove home. "There's nothing wrong with you! This is just a trick to get out of school!"

It wasn't a trick. Something horrible was happening and Will didn't know what it was.

After his mother went back to work, Will threw up his breakfast. Then he fell asleep on the couch in the living room, even though the TV was blaring.

The nightmare returned.

The black cloud over his face grew thicker and heavier, and poured into him so fast that he choked.

He woke up with a picture in his mind of a face, half human, half wildcat. It had glowing yellow eyes and sharp pointed teeth.

This picture stayed with him. It haunted him, even after he'd woken up. It wouldn't go away. Every time he closed his eyes he could see it, coming out of the blackness, hissing and snarling.

Chapter 6

OUT OF SIGHT

Melissa was on her way to Will's house when she saw Mrs. Noonan's car drive by. Will's mother was at the wheel and Will was sitting in the front next to her. They looked like they were arguing about something.

Melissa hid behind a telephone pole and waited until the car was gone. It looked like Mrs. Noonan was home for the day, taking care of Will. So Melissa couldn't go visit him after all.

It was still early, and not many people were out. Melissa made her way back downtown. She headed to the street where the pet store was.

The wildcat was still in the window, prowling slowly back and forth. It looked thinner than ever. The ferret was there, too, but the lizard and the snake were gone.

The inside of the store was just as dark and quiet as it had been four days earlier. The sign on the door had faded a little.

Melissa tried the door. It wasn't locked.

She took a deep breath and went inside.

The smell was so strong that she almost gagged. It was a warm, sweet, rotten smell, like something had died somewhere.

A lot of the cages were empty.

There was no sign of the old man anywhere.

The animals that were still there watched Melissa silently.

Melissa stepped forward into the gloom. One of the wildcats lifted up a paw to the front of the cage. It hooked its claws around the thin gray wire.

Melissa walked over to it slowly. "Don't worry," she said. "I'm here to help you. I'm going to set you free."

There was a small wooden door in the corner of each cage.

Melissa walked from one end of the store to the other, opening all the cage doors on the top row.

She went back along the middle row, and finally the bottom, until all the cages were open except for the snake cages.

She left those alone, but she did open up the birdcage to let the parrots out.

Then she went to the window display and opened the three cages there.

None of the animals moved.

"Don't be scared," she said. "I'm not going to hurt you. Go on! Get out of here!"

The animals still didn't move.

Someone might come in at any moment. The old man, or a customer. Melissa started to feel a little scared. She went along the cages again, hitting them with the palms of her hands. "Go!" she yelled. "Get a move on! Look, the door's open! Go!"

From the top row, two wildcats jumped out onto the ground. A ferret streaked behind the counter, out into the back of the shop. Lizards, wildcats, and parrots were scrambling and leaping everywhere.

Melissa turned to go. Then she saw the wildcat from the cage in the window. It was standing directly in front of her. Staring.

It had the yellowest eyes she had ever seen. Weird, evil eyes. And the cat was not scared.

The wildcat came slowly forward, ears flattened, teeth bared. Melissa stepped back. The cat advanced, twitching its tail, watching her. It raised its head.

Then, with a yowl, it ran past her, through the doorway. Then it raced down the street. Soon it was out of sight among the shadows.

Chapter 7

FOOTPRINTS

Will sat on the couch. He couldn't believe it. The pet store. Mr. Brinkley. It was there, right in front of him. On television.

He rubbed his eyes. It must be the fever, making him see weird things. There must be some mistake.

"Local police are still baffled by the death of pet store owner Ron Brinkley, who was found yesterday behind his shop in Green Valley," the reporter said on the television. "According to reports, there was no sign of foul play, and doctors are not sure what happened. Mr. Brinkley lived alone in a house attached to his store, and had very few visitors."

Will's head was spinning. It wasn't true. It couldn't be true. Mr. Brinkley, the man who bit him. He had the same illness Will had now. Mr. Brinkley was dead.

Will lay back on the couch, staring at the TV. Suddenly he understood everything. Everything was perfectly clear.

The bite on his arm. The pet store. The fever. The face that hovered over him in his dreams.

He got up and looked for his baseball cap. Slowly, painfully, he dragged himself out of the house and shuffled up the road toward the main street. The midday sun beat down on him.

When Will reached downtown, he was exhausted. The bright light and the pounding in his head made him dizzy.

He almost gave up, but he couldn't. If what he suspected was true — and it was true, he knew that now — then he couldn't give up. There was only one thing left for him to do.

At the intersection before the stores, he leaned against a traffic light to rest. There was a break in the traffic and he thought he heard a noise behind him. The same strange noise he'd heard four days earlier, down in the Wash. A noise like something growling at him.

Will looked over his shoulder and saw nothing. As he stepped forward, two small shadows appeared, as if by magic, on the sidewalk. The shadows were close behind him. Shadows in the shape of footprints. Walking.

Will stumbled out into the street and was almost run over. The sound of a car horn rang in his ears. He reached the other side of the street and forced himself to keep going, past a gas station and a construction site. In the shade of an awning he stopped and looked behind him again.

The footprints were gone.

Carefully, he stepped out from under the awning into the sun. The footprints reappeared. They looked almost like a human's. Almost, but not quite. Where the toes should have been was something else: the marks of claws.

Will ran, past the bus stop and down the street where the pet store was. As he staggered by the store, he noticed that the door was open. The cages were empty.

There was a lizard basking in sunlight on the sidewalk. That was strange. On the news report he'd seen, the animals had still been there. He was sure of it.

There was no time to think about that.

Ahead of him was the fence that stood above the Wash. The pounding in his head grew louder. The pain in his body got worse.

Will cried out. He stepped forward and prepared to climb the fence. He turned to look for the footprints and saw them glistening in the sunlight. They were darker than before, and closer, much closer. They were only a few feet away.

Somehow he got over the fence and down the other side. That was it. He was trapped inside. He had nowhere left to go.

A heavy weight pressed against his shoulders. A noise like thunder roared in his ears.

The beast face appeared, a mirage shimmering darkly in front of him. Its jaws were wide and gaping. He could see its tongue. Its teeth were white and dripping.

Will fell forward and stumbled headfirst down the bank.

On the valley floor he fell to his knees, gasping.

To his left, the broad, dry riverbed trailed lazily out of town.

Way off in the distance, the mountains loomed. That was where he had to go. He needed to get past the bushes and paths to where the real desert began.

In the desert, there were no people, and no prey. There wasn't anything for the beast thing to feed on.

But the desert was so far away.

Will raised himself, took a step, two steps. The tip of his shoe hit a rock, and he fell.

He tried to get up again but couldn't. The weight on him was too heavy.

It was warm, like an animal, a living creature pressing.

He was starting to pass out. Slipping into blackness.

His mind flowed out of him like water.

Terrified, he thought, I'm not going to make it. I'm not going to.

With a huge effort he turned to look behind him. The footprints were so close he could have touched them.

As he watched, they moved closer, sliding over the stones. He almost laughed when he saw that the footprints were not shadows. They were not shadows at all.

They were alive, and red as blood.

Then Will blacked out and slid to the ground.

Chapter 8

BACK TO THE WASH

Melissa waited until after school, and then went back to Will's house. She knocked on the front door. Will's mother answered. Mrs. Noonan had an apron on over her work clothes and her hands were covered in flour.

Melissa asked to see Will.

"He's not home, I'm sorry," Mrs. Noonan said. "He's supposed to be sick, but he went out somewhere. I don't know where he's gone. Actually, I thought he was with you."

Melissa was quiet for a second. She'd been sure Will would be at home. Something didn't feel right.

"So Will is better? He's not sick?" she asked.

"I guess," Mrs. Noonan said.

Melissa nodded and stood in the door awkwardly. She had a good idea where Will might be. Where did Will always go, when he wanted to be alone?

The Wash.

She mumbled something polite to Mrs. Noonan and left.

It was getting late and the shadows were getting longer. It took Melissa twenty minutes to walk back across town to the boundary fence that circled the Wash.

Then it took another five minutes to find the trail that led down the bank to the stones.

When she was sure she had the right spot, she climbed to the other side. Halfway down the track she found a broken branch and a cotton thread hanging from a bush.

Farther down, there were more broken branches and spots of dried blood on the ground. It could be human blood, or it could be animal blood. Melissa wasn't sure.

She thought of all the wildcats she had let out, afraid and half starved. Then she hurried down the hill to the riverbed.

A few feet from the bank she found Will's baseball cap, lying among the stones.

Just the baseball cap; nothing else. No sign of Will.

The strange thing about the cap was that it was lying upriver from the trail. Away from the town.

It was as though Will had been heading north, out toward the mountains.

That was crazy.

Nobody ever went that way, not even the older kids who came down here when they skipped school. There was no shade, no relief from the sun, and nothing to see except desert.

She picked up the cap and looked at it. The wind must have blown it, she decided. It must have gotten blown back along the riverbed.

She began walking back toward the town.

Up ahead of her, past where the river turned, she could see the main highway bridge carrying traffic through the town. Another smaller bridge arched beside it.

All around her in the valley were rocks and dead trees. Clumps of desert grass. Piles of old building materials. Closer, jutting out of the far bank in the early evening shadows, was the storm drain.

Melissa made her way forward and peered in between the pillars. Nothing.

She looked up the bank into the bushes, where Will sometimes liked to climb. Nothing there either.

Just as she was about to leave she thought she heard a scraping noise. It sounded muffled, like it was inside something. It sounded like it was coming from the storm drain.

She walked around to the front and peered inside. It was dark in there and smelled moldy.

A black slime covered the concrete. Besides the slime, Melissa couldn't see anything at all.

"Will?" she called. "Will, is that you?"

There was no sound for a moment. Then she heard something coming from the inner darkness. It sounded like a cough.

In a voice hardly more than a whisper, Will answered her. "No! Melissa! Don't . . . come . . . !"

"Will, it's me!" Melissa said. "Listen, I have something to tell you. I went back to the pet store today and let all the animals out! Isn't that amazing?"

There was no answer at all this time. Just a long silence. Melissa lifted herself into the mouth of the drain and crawled forward.

Inside the drain, the air was hot and damp. Her knees kept slipping on the black slime.

As her eyes got used to the light she thought she saw something.

There was a shape just up ahead of her. It was like a crouching, dark shadow.

Was it Will? It had to be. Why didn't he speak?

"It was so great, you wouldn't believe it," she went on. "There was nobody in the store, so I just opened up the cages and let them out. The lizards and parrots and everything. And about a dozen wildcats. Including that one in the window. You remember that one?"

Melissa paused, waiting for an answer.

Then she went on. "Boy, it had the yellowest eyes. You should've — Will? Hey, what's the matter? Why are you looking at me like that? Will . . . ?"

ABOUT THE AUTHOR

Jonathan Harlen was born in New Zealand and has worked as a scriptwriter, comedy writer and journalist, as well as being a well-known writer of children's books. He and his wife now live in Australia, where they own a farm that grows coffee and timber. When Jonathan was growing up, he loved Roald Dahl books. He has three kids.

ABOUT THE ILLUSTRATOR

Tom Jellett has been illustrating books since graduating from the University of South Australia in 1995. He has illustrated a number of picture books and novels. Tom lives in Sydney, Australia, and works as an illustrator for *The Australian*.

GLOSSARY

awning (AW-ning)—a piece of fabric, metal, or wood that sticks out from a building to shade it from sun and keep out rain

coiled (KOY-uhld)—wrapped in a series of loops

exhausted (eg-ZAWS-tid)—very tired

ferret (FARE-it)—a long, thin animal that is related to the weasel

paradise (PARE-uh-dyss)—a perfect place

plague (PLAYG)—a terrible disease, especially one that is easily passed from one person to another

rural (RUR-uhl)—having to do with the countryside

smog (SMOG)—a mixture of fog and smoke that sometimes hangs in the air over cities and factories

swollen (SWOHL-in)—made larger

temperature (TEM-pur-uh-chur)—a measurement of how warm something is

DISCUSSION QUESTIONS

1. This book is called *The Plague*. A plague is a terrible disease that one person can pass to another. Do you think this is a good title for the story? Why or why not?

2. Why is Melissa so upset by the animals in the store's windows? Why does she let them all out?

3. What do you think happens at the end of this book? What happens to Will and Melissa?

WRITING PROMPTS

1. In this book, Will goes to the Wash when he wants to be alone. Do you have a special place where you go when you need time to yourself? Describe it.

2. We know that Will got sick when Mr. Brinkley bit him. But how did Mr. Brinkley get sick? Write a list of possibilities.

3. At the beginning of this book, Melissa and Will decide not to go to school. Instead, they go to the Wash. What would you do if you unexpectedly had a day off of school?

TAKE A DEEP BREATH AND

Janet never had a friend before Lola came along. When Lola asks her to sleep over, Janet jumps at the chance. She takes the bus to the Half Moon Bridge, where Lola promised to meet her. Lola doesn't show up . . . but a strange dog does.

STEP INTO THE SHADE!

When Jenna reads a weird book about a mysterious cure for old age, she wants to try it out. The main ingredient is fish guts, so she tries it on her parents first. But she doesn't know that these fish guts have a very strange effect on humans.

INTERNET SITES

Do you want to know more about subjects related to this book? Or are you interested in learning about other topics? Then check out FactHound, a fun, easy way to find Internet sites.

Our investigative staff has already sniffed out great sites for you!

Here's how to use FactHound:

1. Visit *www.facthound.com*
2. Select your grade level.
3. To learn more about subjects related to this book, type in the book's ISBN number: **1598898612**.
4. Click the **Fetch It** button.

FactHound will fetch the best Internet sites for you!